Love
RAMADAN

A NOVELLA BY
TOHIB ADEJUMO

LOVE IN RAMADAN ©TOHIB ADEJUMO

This novel is a work of fiction. Any references to real people, events, establishments, or locales are intended only to give the fiction a sense of reality and authenticity. Other names, characters, and incidents occurring in the work are either the product of the author's imagination or are used factiously, as are those fictionalized events and incidents that involve real persons. Any characters that happens to share the name of a person who is an acquaintance of the author, past or present, is purely coincidental and is in no way intended to be an actual account involving that person.

ISBN: 978-0-692-57694-6

For wholesale pricing, event bookings, and all other inquiries email: tohibadejumo@gmail.com

Praises for *Love In Ramadan*

I recommend this novella to anybody who wants to have a feel of the mind of immigrants in America... ...they will relate to the story and have a little kick out of the African mannerisms well depicted by Adejumo's crafty writing skills.

---- Papatia Feauxzar, the author of Steadfast.

Tohib gives readers front row seats into the minds of the American children of Nigerian immigrants, and he explains so many important issues in Islam in the easiest and most beautiful manner.

---- Tope Ganiyat Fajingbesi, Public Speaker and Radio Host, Impact Africa.

I recommend this book, if I could describe it in one word, I would say: deep. I felt so many emotions as I delved deeper into Malik's life (a Nigerian-American Muslim student). Love, one of the book's main themes, is a universal thing.

---- Nusaibah Martha, Baccalaureate in linguistics and religious studies.

I only wish that more people in America could read stories like [this] so they could drop their deeply misguided fear of what I believe (and is shown in the book) is a beautiful, life-giving set of beliefs and accompanying culture.

---- Jane Elliot, Associate Professor of Theatre, City University of New York.

...snarky and smooth jokes in the novella. And small traces of *dawah* that weren't preachy at all.
---- Hayati Magazine

Acknowledgements

All gratitude belongs to Almighty God. May the peace and blessings of God be upon all the Messengers of God.

I thank my grandmother, Alhaja Falilatu Sanusi Adejumo, for raising me. And I am grateful to my parents for the gift of life. I thank my professors at Borough of Manhattan Community College who assigned papers that gave me migraines but also increased my writing skills. I'm especially grateful to Dr. Jean Arrington, Dr. Rose Kim, and Dr. Paula Saunders for their readiness to always assist and engage me both inside and outside of the classrooms. I'm also grateful for the impact Dr. Fozea Fryddie has had on my life.

I thank Adam and Muzameel for encouraging me to write this story. My utmost gratitude goes to Nusaiba and Hajarah for polishing this manuscript, and to Zara J for helping me turn the manuscript into a book. I thank Aminat, Suliya, and Sumbo for their feedbacks and words of encouragement which reinforced my commitment during stressing times. I also thank Uncle Ismail for his help and support.

I thank Sahid, my brother and friend, for his moral, emotional and financial support. Sahid, thanks a lot for being my strength and for being the best big brother in the world.

Above all, I am grateful to Zaynab, my wife, for being my repose against the strains of the outside world. Zaynab, thank you so much for giving me peace; thank you for your patience and understanding, thank you for loving me, and last but definitely not the least, thank you for marrying me.

To Zaynab,

> For your love and gentleness and for allotting
> the characters in this book your own portions of
> my days.

To Nabintou and Fatimah,

> For your courage and strength

To Khalimmat, Nadia, and Yesirat,

> You gems know too well why ☺

And to you, the Reader,

> Thank you!

Ta'ni mo se?

Who did I wrong?

Stand clear of the closing doors, please. The automated voice cautioned as a man and his son in Yankee shirts rushed out just before the door closed. I stood and offered my seat to a frail looking lady in a distressed orange jacket who had just boarded the train. She at first refused, but I told her I was getting off at the next stop. "*Gracias mi hijo,*" she said, and held onto the pole before sitting. I looked at an African woman sitting alone beside the door, and my parents came to mind.

I already knew that my parents would be shocked, especially my mother. She would probably explode when she hears, but in life, one has to just let somethings out, even if they might be received negatively. When I got to my stop on the number 4 express train, I made up my mind and decided to bite the bullet once and for all. I was going to tell my parents.

Ambience swept over me as the train galloped away from the 167th street train station. From the overhead metal bars, I took a look down at the busy intersection and something I hadn't felt in about four months crept into me. African immigrant merchants' tables laden with socks, phone chargers, wallets among other things sat by the sidewalks. A couple of African American men stood by the intersection, in one's hands were bottles of water and the other was shooting bubbles from a plastic toy gun. A Hispanic lady pushed her ice cream truck to a halt, and looked at two white ladies who had apparently been directed to buy ice cream by two boys holding their hands. That feeling of being in New York City, the diverse city, the bustling city, returned to me that spring noon after four months of intense studying at Ithaca.

I walked up to Morris Avenue where Al Irshad Muslim Society Mosque was. My hands buried in my grey Burberry jacket, and my gaze all over the place, taking in the sights of pawn shops, African markets, hair braiding salons, grocery stores as well as the eccentricities of people tarrying about the mildly scorching sun. It was late May, summer was already knocking at the door. People were still wearing jackets though; as it sometimes got extremely cold in the ebbing days of spring. When I got close to the mosque, I heard the voice of Imam Abdul Rahman reciting some of the dhikr we recited in Asalaatu. I took in a large dose of oxygen on hearing his voice and rubbed my hands on my face. I opened the green door of the building and took the staircase to the second floor where the cozy mosque was.

The sight which greeted me was nothing less than colorful. The door to the mosque put me in the middle of the congregation where to my right were men dawned in different clothes. Some wore buba made of ankara or lace fabric, others wore white jallabiya, while some were in shirts and trousers. To my left were the most beautiful people in my world— Yoruba Muslim women— attired in rich lace and colorful ankara iro and buba, few among them wore abayah, dainty long scarves complementing most of the elder women's dresses. On the much younger ladies, there seemed to be a preference for ankara skirts and blouses and the use of thicker scarves. I walked straight to the door adjacent to the entrance, and made my way to the rest room, where I made wudu.

Coming back from the rest room, I bumped into Alhaja Sekinat, the vice president of the female wing of Al-Irshad Muslim society. She had on a yellow lace iro and buba, her head covered with a white slightly transparent scarf, with it she wore a gold necklace, and her earrings were glittering. I bent and greeted her.

"How are you, Malik?" she asked, patting my left shoulder.

"I'm fine, ma." I responded with a half-smile.

"And how was school? Hope you did well as expected?"

"Alhamdulillah—praise be to God, ma. I did my best."

"I'm sure you did, but you have lost a lot of weight. Is it school that made you lose so much weight?"

I couldn't answer that question so I just let it pass and smiled in response. It was true that I had become lean and I wasn't dieting nor had I planned to lose weight. Not that I had been fat before going to school, rather I was normal size—whatever that means— but by the time the spring semester bade farewell, my pants, which hitherto did not care for zipping, started to appeal for belts. The spring semester of my first year at Cornell University proved to be more strenuous than the fall I matriculated. There were more papers to write and more difficult subjects to embrace.

"Greet your mother for me," she resumed, "and tell her that Alhaja Arike's daughter is getting married and we have chosen lace and *gele* (head-tie). Tell her that altogether the cost is two hundred dollars.''

"I will, ma.''

I entered into the mosque and sat on the floor, its fluffy surface rug welcoming me. I noticed that it was not the same rug we used to have before I left for school. The new rug was green and had mosque imprint on it. I joined the dhikr session, reciting the last ten chapters of the Qur'an and after that, the Imam instructed one of the young alfas—typically those who just came from Nigeria—to recite the supplication which is referred to as *khutbah* among the Nigerian Muslim community and as *qunut* among other communities. After the supplication, the Imam gave the floor to the members for testimonies or special prayers. Aminat, a seven year old girl, walked to the front and deposited a fifty dollar bill inside a stainless steel bowl in front of the Imam. She bent and tilted her head towards the imam, whispering in his ear, and then returned to the back where the women sat.

Imam Abdul Rahman held the cordless microphone close to his mouth, making his leather wrist watch apparent under the 'hand' of his white agbada, and announced, "Alhaja Adekola said we should use this fifty dollar to thank Allah for her daughter who just gained admission into Harvard University."

It was common for people at the mosque to show gratitude to God in such a way. Birthdays, graduations, green card attainment, and other joyous happenings are normally followed by such gesture in Nigerian Muslim community, especially among the Yorubas. Even when people's aged parents die, such a gesture also ensues. The Imam made prayer for everyone who laid down money for special request, and at the end, he prayed for the entire congregation and enjoined the members to be more punctual at

Asalaatu and to make sure to leave time out for Friday prayer. The public relations officer then stood to make announcements, but by that time, the women section of the mosque had become a minimarket. I went to greet Imam Abdul Rahman and he asked about school and other stuffs, then he prayed for me.

I stood outside the mosque, waiting for my friend, Raqeeb. He and I were close while in high school but our correspondence went to all time low as soon as he left for Albany and I Ithaca. We only said hi to each other throughout the semester a couple of times on Facebook. I was holding on to the black metal gate of the building's fence when my gaze fell on the just arriving B42, and the passengers alighting from it. An old man pushed his walker toward the bus, taking all the time in the world to get there. And I was glad to see that the bus driver waited.

"Ha ha ha.'' The sound came from my rear and I turned to see Alhaja Olaide. Her broad face exhibited too much application of foundation and powder and her lips bore witness to a meticulous glossing of lipstick. Alhaja Olaide enjoyed fashion and always looked

7

beautiful. Her gele colors always matched with her handbags.

"*Eyin ara* upstate, you have returned from school?"

That's one of the strange ways our parents speak. If I hadn't returned from school, how would I be standing in front of her? I laughed and told her I had indeed returned.

"How was school?" She enveloped her arm over me, her emerald lace brushing my jacket, and her scent filtering into my nose.

"School was fine," I replied, my head bent.

"That's my boy, I'm sure you aced all your classes," she commented and then released me. "Your sister," referring to her daughter even though we had no family ties, "says she has started summer class and couldn't come home. You kids see each other at school, right?" I averted my gaze from her and nodded that we do see each other. "She is so busy with studies these days," she said more to herself than to me.

"Yes she is.'' A lump developed in my throat and I almost choked commenting.

Alhaja Olaide dipped into her green handbag and handed me two new twenty dollar bills, telling me to use that for my transport fare back to Brooklyn. "Tell your mother that I said she should feed my son," she ordered, her black Toyota Rav4 door coming unlocked.

Raqeeb didn't come out on time so I started strolling down 167th street toward the train station. Dusk had begun to conceal the sky when I walked up the staircase and sat on one of the platform's wooden benches. The electronic board in green colors read seven minutes for the next 4 train. As I sat alone on the platform that Sunday evening, cold wind blew over my jacket, and I ruminated over the praise Alhaja Olaide had heaped on her daughter, Damola. Obviously, she told her mother she had started summer class even though summer class wasn't starting until the middle of June.

Damola was a fellow Cornelius. She was in her senior year and we had known each other since the commencement of Al Irshad as both our parents were among the pioneers of the association. She was to all people at the mosque a good girl, but when I got to Cornell, what I saw and heard of her was very disheartening. Although I didn't expect to see her in hijab or something, every time I saw her on campus, she always dressed sassy. And on one night, after having been practically forced by my dorm mates to a night club, I saw her getting wasted by the bartender resulting in her being hobbled out by her friends. One time, a sex tape was leaked in school and I was ashamed to the core when my friends showed me my kinswoman as part of the lurid tape that went viral among students.

This wasn't a peculiar thing. Many of my friends to varying degrees do similar things. It was a problem of multiple personalities that plagued the first generation of Nigerian American Muslims of which I was a part of. We showed one face at home and showed another at school. In my assessment, right from the beginning of our lives, we had been brewed to having two personalities. One for the mosque, the Asalaatu, the Arabic school; and the other was for schools, parties, and other "secular functions." So, for example, one might see a parent command his or her daughter to wear hijab while coming to the mosque, and the same parent would buy the daughter a mini skirt or a backless gown for a picnic. With this kind of mindset, we internalized the binary view of life where we followed the laws of the Qur'an while at mosque and defied those same laws outside the mosque.

Later that night, I sat with my mother at the dining area, my mind lost in deep thoughts. I heard footsteps behind me and then felt a mild knock on my head. I turned my head and my father's smiling but weary face greeted me.

"I heard you went to Asalaatu today," he said as he drew a chair out.

"Yes, I did and Imam told me to greet both of you."

He nodded and by this time, white rice and spicy stew on porcelain plates had materialized, staring daringly at us. My mother dashed out turkey meats and after each had said bismillah, we began eating, and talking. My father started the conversation by asking about my grades and I told him that I got A's in three courses and that I was waiting for the other two to be posted. I remembered what both Alhaja Sekinat and Olaide had charged me to tell my mother so I told her someone was getting married (I had forgotten the name) and that she needed to feed me.

When we finished eating, my father asked me about the semester because since Friday, when I got home, we hadn't had the chance to sit and talk. I was glad he brought up the issue of school because I had been considering talking to him and my mother about my decision. I called my mother who was by the sink, washing the plates we just finished using, to join us. She closed the faucet and walked back to the dining area, her hair disheveled, and her eyes bloodshot.

"Hope no problem, Malik? You look serious, like something is troubling your mind," my father asked after removing a toothpick from his mouth.

"Daddy, school was really hard this semester," I began, but my mother cut in.

"*Oko mi,* we understand that but the end will be worth it. Soon you will become a doctor and will forget the hard days."

I was a bit infuriated by her statement that they understood what I was going through but seemed not to care. I got angry but kept my composure.

"Mom, dad, I know you want the best for me but there are some issues I need to decide for myself."

"Why are you talking like this, Malik?" my father asked, confusion splashed all over his face. Concern was also palpable on my mother's countenance and because I knew it would hurt them, I almost backed out from telling them that night. "Whatever it is, you can tell us," my father encouraged.

"Mom, dad, I have decided not to return to Cornell for my sophomore year. I want to stay in the City with you and go to school here."

My mother's face grew red and she roared a host of rhetorical questions, none of which I understood. She turned to Yoruba and said I would go back whether I liked it or not. I buried my head and refused to meet her gaze. My father was silent but even though I didn't look at him, I still could feel the intense disappointment oozing out from him. My mother clapped her hands incessantly and hissed numerous times while pacing around the dining area. Then she suddenly stopped, and then asked, "Ta'ni mo se?"

Eebi'o paa' e
You are not hungry

I was in the living room watching Desperate Housewives when my mother purposely came and crushed my quiet, soothing afternoon. She sat on the loveseat, adjacent to where I was, and dialed her big sister's number who was in Nigeria. They exchanged normal pleasantries, talked about family matters, and gossiped about a relative who refused to work but expected them to give him money. At first, the phone was glued to her cheek but as the conversation continued she placed the phone on the center table and put it on speaker. Her shawl falling from her shoulder, she immersed her hands into her braids, undoing them.

"My sister, please save me," she said in Yoruba.

I was taken aback, confused. What context did that come from? Even my aunty was muddled.

"What's wrong Iya Malik?"

"It is Malik o, my sister. I don't know what has come over him."

"Malik?" My aunt asked.

"Yes o," my mother replied, "he doesn't want to go to school anymore."

That wasn't true. I said I wasn't going to Cornell anymore, not I wasn't going to school. I imagined my aunt furrowing her brows and putting her hands over her chest as I had often in similar cases seen my mother do. They both went back and forth on me, each bringing about her own theories for my decision and after their lengthy discussion, which involved the raising of voices, they both concluded there was more to my issue than what initially met the eyes.

"It's not eyes only," my aunt said, suggesting a metaphysical influence.

"I thought as much," mother affirmed. "*Sista mi,* please go out on this issue and do not let my effort on Malik become fruitless."

My aunt kept silent for a while, then said, "Put your mind at rest. I'm on it. I will go to Alfa Jamiu's place and find out what's wrong."

15

I couldn't help but wonder how they both thought visiting a cleric in Lagos would change my mind towards Cornell. My heartbeat rose and veins stood, but I didn't allow my ego to get the better of me. I pressed the off button on the remote control and went to my room.

For a whole week, my mother refused to speak with me. We would pass by each other in the house and a single word wouldn't be battered. My father and I had few nights where he tried to persuade me but I was resolute. The following Saturday, I returned from the mosque between Empire Boulevard and Nostrand Avenue where I had biked to for the Isha' prayer to find that my mother hadn't returned home. I was pleased to this knowledge because sitting in the living room wouldn't be suffocating as it had been on Monday.

I sat down and put the plasma TV to work. I surfed the channels but none of the programs caught my attention; so I shut it off. I went to the kitchen, opened the freezer— lo and behold! — a bowl of almond vanilla ice cream. I returned to the living room and sat on the loveseat, my right leg on the glass center table and the ice cream bowl in my hand. I dipped in a strong plastic spoon and melted the cold cream on my tongue, followed by the chewing of the almond. Life doesn't get better than that, I remember thinking that night. But the thought of my mother not speaking with me visited me and I started to see things from her perspective. She couldn't understand my abrupt change, and I knew the majority of Nigerian parents wouldn't understand my decision either, if placed in my mother's shoes. After all, I was exceptionally brilliant.

Tuition payment was not a problem as I had a full scholarship and passing wasn't a problem either as God blessed me with brilliancy. But, you see, the problem was my mental well-being and most importantly the concern for my soul. Like I said, I had a full scholarship but like other scholarships, it came with conditions. One of the conditions stipulated that I must take the minimum of fifteen credits each semester and I must not get lower than 3.8 grade point average. The fifteen credit per semester wasn't a problem, but, even for someone as brilliant as I was, to maintain a 4.0 in Cornell was an arduous and daunting task. Professors were allowed to give A's to no more than a quarter of the class, so to keep the perfect GPA, one had to work as though one's life depended on it. The first semester I got a 4.0, and I also got the same thing came spring, but for the latter I worked too hard. There were sometimes when I felt like I was floating on a river, alone, in the wilderness. I would spend days and nights studying, hours and hours writing research papers, and having little time to rest or actually live.

There was an instance when I had to rewrite my English 201 research paper thrice. What happened was I chose a topic and wrote up to ten pages, but then I suddenly felt the topic wasn't good, so I embarked on a new one. I wrote the new one up to seven pages then found it to be wanting coherence, so I threw it out. I felt the same way about the last one but at that point I couldn't write anything anymore. I recalled one chilly night, in pajamas, a coffee mug in my hand, standing on the balcony of my twenty-fifth floor dorm and asking myself what the point of all the stress was. I wanted to quail my stress, but I had no idea how to. It was completely overwhelming. I was overwhelmed.

A week before the paper was due, I ran behind Professor Wilson that morning as the class was concluded. "I need to talk to you," I alerted the professor.

"Sure," he replied, as he continued to thrust papers into his briefcase. "When would you like to come and see me? During my office hours?" His eyes blinking behind his glasses.

"I was hoping we could talk now," I said, taking out my course folder from my bag which was now on the floor.

"Now?" His eyebrows raised. "Malik, I have…."

I did not allow him the chance to finish but spread in front of him three research papers I had written. "I feel like none of them are good enough to earn me an A," I confessed.

He took the papers from me and surveyed them briefly, he then told me to choose one for him to check. I chose the one I wrote last and we parted. I received an email from him that night where he said my paper was good and that I should take things easy.

I didn't know what had evaporated all the ice cream when I looked into the bowl. I knew I was enjoying every journey of the spoon to my mouth but precisely what had catalyzed the demise of the ice cream, I couldn't say. My phone gave out a sound and when I checked what it was, it turned out to be Jenn, my ex-girlfriend. She posted a photo of us on her Facebook wall and tagged me in it. In the photo, Jenn sat on my thighs and her friend, Caroline, alongside Joshua, my friend, took their places on our sides. A wide grin creased my mouth, in the photo, my gaze toward Jenn whose white teeth met the camera. I smiled at the remembrance of the lust filled days during the early weeks of spring. I wanted more of that and in Ithaca it was almost impossible for me not to get it. Jenn was a white girl with blond hair. We met at the orientation for new students and became close over the semesters. We didn't quite break up, but when I started to take my belief in Islam seriously, I knew I had to cut down on our relationship.

My parents meant well. They wanted me to graduate from an Ivy League school and become a doctor. I wanted that too but not at the expense of my sanity (as I believed another semester may push me into depression). My father was a cabdriver and my mother a nurse. They'd both, to varying degrees, gave up their dreams to give me a better life, and for that, I was grateful. My mother was especially serious about me becoming a doctor as this, I suspected, would give her the pleasure of living her dreams through me, her only child. She had wanted to become a medical doctor herself but because of financial burdens here and back home in Nigeria, she had settled for a career in nursing.

The door opened and my mother entered into the living room, grocery bags in both her hands. I heaved and rushed to take them from her.

"How are you?" and with that our boycotting of each other came to an end.

"I'm fine," I replied, now walking to the kitchen.

She followed and told me to put one of the bags in the sink. She stood by the sink and opened the plastic bag. Fresh chicken thighs and wings surfaced. I sat by a chair facing the sink, and we started to talk, her back fronting me.

"Mom, I like this your uniform, it looks good on you."

"You like it?" she asked, now rinsing the chicken under the faucet. "I was tired of all the colored uniforms so I thought I should try white."

"That chicken is from African Market, right?"

"Yes, why?"

"You know they sell halal chicken there. You see, chicken on the free market are not slaughtered in a good way so I don't want to be eating them anymore."

"*Eebi o ti pa'e ni yen,*" she replied as she walked to place a pot on the cooker. I smiled.

For a few minutes, the kitchen was silent except for the clinking of the microwave. It was apparent that the issue of my school hovered around the kitchen and I became worried that our truce would expire soon. I tried to say something but I didn't know what to say that wouldn't bring about that dreaded confrontation. I was about to say something when my mother spoke to me, "I saw your wife,

Raliat, today." My expression didn't change and it turned out my mom had been expecting it to. When she saw that I didn't say anything, "Will you not get angry for me calling her your wife?" she asked.

I began to laugh and she shook her head. "You both have become adults, *abi*? I said the same thing to her and she just laughed."

Raliat was my childhood friend and her parents' house used to be right next to ours. We went to PS 92 together and were in the same grade even though she was a year older. We used to spend so much time together at each other's houses that our parents and other people used to tease us by calling us husband and wife. I used to get furious when people called me Raliat's husband during those years of childhood, I just didn't grasp that humorous call— one of the adults' eccentricities I couldn't understand then.

"I saw her at work," my mother resumed, "she's now working as a food service worker at our hospital."

"That's nice," I commented, sounding as nonchalant as possible.

"What's nice?" mother began. "She shouldn't be working. It will affect her school and moreover I don't understand why her mother didn't make her go and study outside the city."

I knew since the conversation had drifted into something about school, it would not be long before the inevitable confrontation ensued. So, I kept quiet and let my mother vent about the need to school outside the city. But inside me, anger brew as she kept on blaming Raliat's mom for not paying enough attention to Raliat and her little sister. What she wanted them to do, I couldn't lay my hands on. She knew just as I did the delinquency which threw Raliat and her family's lives off balance and yet she was blaming Raliat's mother.

We were in the junior year of high school when we returned home to find men in dark stuffy black suits in front of their house. Her mother was standing on the porch, talking to two of the guys in suits, one with a briefcase and the other showing some kind of document to Raliat's mother whose visage displayed anguish as the men explained things to her. We couldn't make out what they were telling her because we were a block away, but we knew it couldn't be good. Two weeks later, the house was locked up.

Raliat, her mother, and little sister had to stay with us for a while. Her father at that time was in the hospital. A few weeks later, on an afternoon, we were in the living room watching TV when my mother came from work and, after sitting close to Raliat and putting her arms over her, told her that her father had passed. I will never forget that haunting image of sadness spreading its mat all over Raliat's face. Raliat and her little sister a few weeks later left for Nigeria where they would live for three years, leaving only their mother behind in New York. Months later, I learnt the reason behind all their tumult. The FBI had charged Raliat's father to court on money laundering charges and the IRS had also fined him $45,000 for tax evasion or something like that.

"Malik," my mother called. I raised my head and saw that she was now facing me. My heart began pounding. "You say you don't want to go to Cornell anymore because of stress?"

I nodded in response.

She fixed her gaze at me, and I saw a tinge of sadness in her eyes. "But you still want to be a medical doctor, right?"

"Of course, mommy. I am changing school not my dreams. I can and will still become a medical doctor *In shaa Allah*." I put my hand on her arm in assurance.

"You promise?" her eyes twinkling, a sign of imminent rain.

"Yes mom, I promise," I quickly said hoping to avert the change in weather.

But I was too late. The next thing I knew I was in her arms, and tears began to fall on my shirt. My father knew how to walk, as our elders usually say. He walked in at that moment and joined our hug. It was of immense joy to see both of them support me, but as providence would have it, another turbulence awaited us that summer.

Osu alapanle

The Noble Month

I was sitting on the bed in my dorm and Raqeeb was there with me. There was a video game console on a stool near the window and our hands gripped the game controllers firmly. Then someone dashed in, without knocking. It was Layla, Raliat's little sister, on her head sat a huge gele. She looked more grown. I asked her what she was doing in my room, and she rolled her eyes.

"This is our house," she said, and jumped on the bed. And the next thing I knew, the room was now the living room of their old house from which they were evicted.

Raliat came in, walking gently and as she got closer and closer, I realized it was not her anymore, it was Jenn. Jenn wore a pink t-shirt and tight black pants. She flashed a smile at me, then started hitting the table, which was now a class desk with a baton in her hand. The sound kept disturbing me until I opened my eyes to know that someone was knocking on my door.

"Malik, wake up. It's almost time for *sahur*." My father announced behind the door.

That's when I realized it was time for the first predawn meal of that year's Ramadan.

I went into the bathroom, and after easing myself, I stood by the sink to make wudu'. I splashed water on my face and its coolness was soothing and rejuvenating. I stared at my reflection in the mirror, and for the first time, I realized and acknowledged the semblance between my mother and me. I looked exactly like her as people used to say all the time. It was an immense pleasure knowing that my mother wasn't angry at me again; for even though my father seemed more understanding than she was, there was this profound bond I had developed with my mother which I didn't have with my father.

I was in the sixth grade and I used to have frequent nosebleeds. One day the bleeding got so intense that it led to a serious migraine which in turn resulted in me losing consciousness. I was rushed to a hospital in Brooklyn where I stayed for two weeks before the doctors decided I had to have surgery. My father was on a vacation in Nigeria then, so the burden of my ailment fell wholly on my mother's shoulders.

Waking up after the surgery, the first person I saw was my mother. She was sitting on a chair, her head resting on my bed, close to my hand. "Mom," I mustered all the strength to speak.

"Oko mi," she exclaimed in a low voice, "you're awake, thank you God." Her eyes spoke dozens. She was excited but still worried. She was awake, but her eyes were blood. "Malik, my little husband, have mercy on me. You know you're the only one I have."

I smiled at her and told her I was fine. "I'm thirsty," I said, turning my head towards her. She jumped out to get water instantly.

It was the Ramadan that propelled my world into real spirituality and religiosity. The month of fasting fell into the hottest and lengthiest days of summer that year. We fasted from mid-June till mid-July. It was brisk hot throughout, but Muslims understood that their lives were to be in servitude to God so we didn't let that deter us. The first night of Ramadan I prayed tarawih at Masjid Taqwa at the intersection of Fulton Street and Bedford. It was a beautiful tarawih, the mosque was jam-packed, as believers from all walks of life and backgrounds lined in rows in devotion to the Lord of the Worlds. I had gotten my license at upstate so that afforded me the opportunity to drive my mother's white Chevrolet car around.

The second night, I moved my compass upwards and decided to visit Masjid Tajjul Huda, the mosque of Imole Adini Muslim Society in the Bronx. When I was young, my father used to take me to the mosque on weekends because the Arabic school there was strong. I had a couple of friends there too but I never really took an interest in going there afterwards. In fact, I never really liked to go to any Asalaatu until after my first year at college when I had a spiritual awakening. That night, however, I went there in order to enjoy the recitations of some children who had just returned from Egypt as eloquent reciters of the Qur'an. And I wasn't disappointed. The recitation was so good that I didn't want the tarawih to end. After the prayer, I stood outside the mosque, and waited for Raliat who had promised to bring me some books.

A week before Ramadan, Raliat and I had bumped into each other at Istijabah Mosque in Brooklyn. It was close to eleven o'clock at night. I had driven my mother who wanted to join the congregation in their recitation of the entire Qur'an in a sitting, a tradition repeated at the end of every month. I had dropped my mother and driven off to find a parking spot three blocks away from the mosque. While returning, I chatted away with one of my friends from Ithaca, and the next thing I knew I bumped into her.

"O' I'm sorry," I apologized without lifting my gaze to know who I had collided into.

"It's okay," she shrugged, "I wasn't looking too."

It had been three years since we last saw each other but I had not a single trouble knowing that it was her, hearing her soft voice. "O' it's you, Malik," she exclaimed about the same time I mentioned her name.

"How long has it been?" I asked after retreating a few steps from her.

"Well, it has been over three years now," she replied, her hand fixing her hijab pin.

"Are you just getting here?" I asked but her phone rang before she could answer and she told me to excuse her. She walked gently away from the lighted anterior of the mosque, where the recitation going on inside escaped to the ears of people on the sidewalk, and she moved towards a closed deli shop where the light was dimmer. In about a minute, she walked back to the front of the mosque.

"That was my mom," she said as she inserted her phone back into a green purse in her hand.

"She's worried?" I grinned.

"O' yes! She is. She wanted to know if I had gotten to the Tahajud and when I would be returning home."

I didn't know where they now lived because ever since she got back from Nigeria we had never engaged that much. "How far is your place from here?" I demanded, toying with my phone so as not to meet her gaze.

"We now live in Harlem.''

I told her if she didn't mind, I could drive her home since the recitation wouldn't end until around one o'clock in the morning, and she said she would appreciate it. We didn't join the congregation in the mosque that night, rather we sat on the door step of the closed deli and talked into the night.

We brought our discussion to an end only when people started egressing the mosque. I went inside the mosque and claimed my portion of the spicy rice Istijabah women are renowned for before going to get the car. I dropped off my mother at home and proceeded with Raliat toward Manhattan. While on the road, we discussed many things and during the course of our discussion three books came out. She told me that they were Islamic novels which had had tremendous effect on her and that she wanted me to read them.

That Ramadan Raliat and I only saw each other twice: the first at Imole Adini and the other time at the Nigerian American Muslim Community (NAMIC) Mosque in Brooklyn. NAMIC was having a fund raising event that night and my father had been one of the special guests. We barely got the chance to talk amid the crowd tightly packed in the mosque. Before my father and I left, I saw her outside and she introduced me to a Latina friend of hers who had just converted to Islam. The sister's name was Patricia. A slender girl with a beautiful frame. She was taller than Raliat but a few inches below my height.

The first book I read was *If I Should Speak* by Umm Zakiyyah. The book resonated with me in that it dealt with college life and the struggles of holding on to one's beliefs. The main character, Tamika, went through trials; debating with herself whether to stay a Christian to please her family or accept Islam and please her Lord. In *A Voice*, its sequel, Sulayman also had to choose between pure academics to the neglect of natural desires or find a way to mitigate between both. And in Umm Juwairiyah's urban Muslim fiction, *The Size of a Mustard Seed,* Jameela too had to decide if she would follow her heart or conform to the shallow expectations of others. So in a subtle way, those fictions prepared me for the dilemma I would fall into as the blessed month began its decline.

But I didn't spend the entire month reading only those novels. I expanded my horizons and got engaged in the remembrance of the Creator by any means which came my way. I followed the leading American Muslim scholars on their Facebook, Twitter, and Instagram pages and listened to their lectures on YouTube. Al Maghrib Institute had a weekend seminar at New York University and I made sure not to miss it. The instructor, Shaykh Yasir Qadhi, was a first generation Pakistani American just like I am Nigerian American. So, when he spoke about Islam and connected the religion with the mundane activities of American life, I felt a kind of connection to his speeches in ways our immigrant scholars had never been able to reach my heart. I subscribed to his page after that seminar and began to enjoy his weekly Seerah Class.

Another scholar I resonated with a lot was Ustadh Nouman Ali Khan of Bayyinah Institute. His specialization was the Qur'an and whenever I listened to his interpretations of the Qur'an that Ramadan, my heart would soar in delight. I would be renewed in my love for the Book of God and would desire nothing more than to put my head on the ground in prostration to my

Creator. Towards the end of the month of blessings, I saw on his Facebook page that he was coming to Queens College to give a lecture, and of course I was there waiting for him when he arrived the night of his lecture. He spoke about the challenges of Muslim youths in America. He touched the issues that were of pressing importance to me such as how to navigate through the demands of college life without losing one's soul in the process. He also cited his personal story and struggle as an undergraduate student in Baruch College during the late nineties. I was amazed when he recounted how he had married his wife at the age of twenty one and how that didn't stop him from reaching his potentials. Ustadh Nouman that night left an indelible impact on my mind.

By the end of Ramadan, I had grown to love and appreciate Islam in a way I had never before. The Qur'an became my friend, and ever since then whenever I have something bothering me, I would turn to God at the end of the day. I would offer the Witr prayer and reflect on words of God through a copy of English Translation of the Qur'an which was on my book shelf, I did this before sleeping at night.

On the twenty seventh night of Ramadan, I was standing in my room on my red praying mat, lights off, and the air condition soothing me with its cool breeze. I stretched my hand out and faced my palm upward as if waiting for God to drop something in them. I threw my heart out and prayed that God guide me to the straight path in both my worldly affairs and that of the hereafter. After that supplication to God, I felt a calmness in me that was too profound and impalpable to put down in words. The calmness transpired into some kind of assurance. From that night onwards, I left my affairs in the hands of God, for He is ever watchful over me.

Ife ni'akoja ofin

Love defies norms

Darkness grew upon the horizon and clouds interlocked over the sky announcing the impending streams of water threatening to let loose. It was a week after Ramadan and Patricia, Raliat, and I had made plans to go to a lecture at Queens. Our rendezvous was to be at the 14th street, Union Square station, but upon getting to the station far too early, I walked down University Place and headed toward the famous white arch of the Washington Square Park. On the way to the park, I passed through the buildings of New York University and I gazed at a building, standing tall over the rest. I wondered how many bodies had thudded on its pavement sidewalk, greeting students who had exhausted hopes about life.

The sidewalks were somewhat clean; two plastic bottles lay beside a garbage can at an intersection.

Two young white men walked past me, their arms defaced with tattoos and on their faces were different kinds of piercings. A lady walked towards a revolving door, tiptoeing as if fearful not to fall in her high heels. Two women stood by the corner of a building, their faces partly covered by the smoke their cigarettes were emitting. I wondered why human beings continued to indulge in blatant self-destructive habits despite our claims to civilization.

I hastened away from Washington Square Park before the torrent began pelting and drenching the roads and humans of Manhattan. Raliat had texted me that she was inside a coffee shop beside Union Square so I went there. When I got inside the coffee shop, I was saddened to see that Patricia was not with Raliat. I had no trouble finding Raliat, as her brown hijab distinguished her from others. She sat at the far end of the shop, close to where the restroom was. I occupied the chair facing her and saw no traces of dampness on her brown ankara dress.

"I guess we cannot go to Queens anymore now?" I asked, chuckling.

"I guess so," she replied, toying with her bracelet which escaped from the covering of her sleeves.

"Patricia couldn't make it anyway," she added. I averted my gaze.

Towards the end of Ramadan, I had begun to think about marriage. It seemed reasonable and logical for me to take that step. I had turned nineteen in May of that year and I needed emotional and physical intimacy just as any other young person. Jenn and I had become history and Islam had become the yardstick for whatever I wanted to do, so having a girlfriend as improvise to having a wife was out of the question. The first person that came to my mind was Raliat but after thinking about our growing up together, the fact that she was older, and the unlikelihood of her having feelings for me, I cast away such fantasy. And also, I wasn't sure if I loved her in the first place.

The caramel skin complexion, the Spanish accent, the long hair, and the zeal of Patricia then hovered over my heart and I began serious consideration of proposing to her. Our going together to Queens even though chaperoned by Raliat, the third wheel, I had planned, would go a long way in affording me the opportunity to engage Patricia and know more about her. I had always had a thing for Hispanics and Latinas since high school, and with Patricia being both Latina and Muslim, she seemed the perfect one for me.

"So you're really not going back to Cornell?"

"Oh no! I'm not. I already applied for a transfer to Hunter College."

Raliat exhaled, sipped coffee, and then set down the brown disposable cup. "I like your decision," she commented.

"You sound like something is on your mind," I suggested.

"Yes, Malik, yes. It's about Layla." My ears perked and I asked what about her. "Layla is going to twelfth grade next session and she wants to go to one of those private schools in upstate. I'm afraid, Malik, I am afraid."

I knew what she was afraid of but right there it seemed to me she needed to vent and me telling her that I understood would not afford her that chance, so I asked what she was scared of.

"You're asking me what I am scared of." Her eyes became wide. "Haven't you been there? Isn't that why you're not going back?" I smiled in response to her questions. "See, Malik, when I came back from Nigeria last year, my plan was to spend two semesters at BMCC, have thirty credits, then transfer to a university upstate. But I am not doing that anymore. It's just too dangerous. Imagine, Layla, all by herself in a town four hours from home, at the prime of her age, attending classes with equally hormone raging guys and girls. What do we expect to happen when her friends or dorm mates tell her to join them in going to parties and nightclubs? Or God forbid, drugs? How is it possible for young people such as ourselves to quell such temptations and not fall headlong into conformity?" She fell silent, took the napkin on her tray and mopped the water forming around her eyelids.

"I know," she resumed, "that these challenges confront students in the city also, but at least it is to a lesser degree. She can stay home if she doesn't want to follow her friends out here in the city, but at school, they could even bring the party to the room or make her feel like an outcast. It's just so hard, and I don't want to lose her.''

"Well, let's just pray to Allah," I managed to comment after sighing.

"Yes, we have to pray," Raliat agreed. "But you know Allah doesn't want us to expose ourselves to fitnah either."

"O' yes, talking of fitnah," she resumed, "do you know how much debt she's going to incur if she goes to those schools? I try to let her see the benefit of getting one's undergraduate degrees at public universities debt free but she is just adamant. I had a professor who went to Brooklyn College for his undergraduate studies, and then did her graduate studies at CUNY Graduate Center, and now she teaches at NYU and City College. She said she's almost without any debt. Isn't that better than incurring debt?"

"It is," I agreed, "but, you know, people are stereotypical about CUNY. I just wish people would come to those Ivy League schools like Cornell and see that the definition of biology there is the same as the one at Medgar Evers College."

By now the torrent had dissipated and I could see that the rain had been relegated to drizzles. I knew the end of the rain would conclude our stay at the coffee shop so I tabled the issue on my mind.

"Patricia," I began, "how well do you know her?"

"Why are you asking?" she inquired as she dusted crumbles of croissant on her chest.

"A friend of mine saw her on Facebook and asked me if I knew more about her."

She took another sip from her coffee and began, "She is a nice sister, *ma shaa Allah.* I have known her for about five months now. We took the same psychology class and that's how we became friends. She has been showing nothing but genuine love for Islam ever since she took her shahadah[*] and is always ready to learn. Her parents were not hard on her for becoming a Muslim, so she lives with them. I don't know what more to say, but yes, she is a nice sister."

The rain came to a halt and we left the coffee shop and headed to the train station. The uptown train arrived as soon as we both swiped our metro cards at

---

[*] Declaration of faith.

the turnstiles and so we bade each other an abrupt goodbye. I stood beside a pillar and watched as Raliat in her lustrous dress paced towards the staircase down the platform amid the crowd of commuters tarrying about Union Square station. And right there something caught my eye.

Later that night, after Isha' prayer, I sat on our porch and gazed at the moon, marveling at the beauty of God's creation. *How could someone see this and not believe in God?* I thought to myself. It was around ten o'clock, so the street was getting placid; the only noises I heard were those of two dogs barking from a distant. My parents were in the living room in each other's arms, one sitting, the other resting on the other's thighs (they seemed to take turns), watching TV. Whenever they're in their *love in Tokyo* mood, I try to grant them their privacy. I opened the can of Vento by my side and wet my dry throat with the cold drink. A few drops trickled down my white shirt and I rubbed the liquid off. I couldn't explain the feeling. It was impalpable. It was as though something ran through my veins and commanded me to take out my phone. I exhaled as I surfed my contacts and dialed her number.

"Hello, salaam alaykum," she greeted me.

"Wa alaykum salaam. Did you get home well?"

"Yes, I did. Thanks. You?"

"Alhamdulillah. I did too." I fell silent for a while.

"Hello? Are you there?"

"Raliat, I have something to ask of you."

"What's that?"

After a moment hesitation I heard myself saying, "I want to marry you."

Baba ati Omo

Father and Son

***You don't expect me to give you an answer this
night, right? I'll think about it.*** Raliat's voice
reverberated in my head as I lay down in my room
surrounded by the forenoon quietness. It had been close
to two weeks and Raliat hadn't said anything about my
proposal to her. The only times we were in contact
during that period was when she liked a status of mine
on Facebook and when she sent Jumuah greetings on
WhatsApp. Other than these, nothing ensued between
us.

It was hot in the room but I didn't want to put the air
condition on so I let myself perspire. I gazed at the white
ceiling and the face of Patricia appeared. What was I
thinking proposing to Raliat instead of Patricia? I
should have known I stood no chance with her. She was
older and more religious. I continued to ruminate about
my decision, reproaching myself for acting on impulse

and not praying Istikharah. But at the very least, Raliat could just act maturely and tell me she isn't interested in someone like me, I began to think, anger boiling in me. What's the silence for? Is she the only woman someone is going to propose to? I kept going back and forth, blaming myself on one hand and getting furious at Raliat on the other. Then my phone sounded. It was Raliat. Her mother wanted to see me.

After praying Jumuah at Masjid Taqwa, I proceeded to Harlem. Their apartment was on the twentieth floor of a building on 137th street. I greeted the security at the lobby, a dark man of heavy frame and robust moustache. I took the elevator by the right of the security's desk. When I got to the twentieth floor, I texted Raliat and in no time she came out of apartment 20 H, just a little to my right.

"Salaam alaykum," she hailed, still standing in front of their door.

"Come on in."

I sat on the nearest couch to the entrance where the view of the apartment could be seen well. The kitchen was to the left of the door, and to the right was a passage that I assumed led to the bathroom and rooms. The living room was small but tastefully designed, a table fan laboring hard to relieve us from heat. Raliat's mother had a nice taste in color: the cream color of the wall matched the light burgundy furniture set and window curtains. I gazed around the room, admiring the family and baby photos on the wall.

In a photo, Raliat and Layla, both very young, wore iro and buba, purple gele decorated their heads. While admiring the room, to my surprise, I realized that Raliat was setting a stool in front of me and placing on it a tray containing a bottle of water and a glass cup. *Me?* My head heaved of flattery. The only times I saw such a thing was in Yoruba movies. *The three years Raliat spent in Nigeria must have changed her.*

I was about to help myself to a sip when Raliat's mother emerged; her sluggish walk suggested she had just woken up from a deep sleep. She sat on the couch to my right, and shot Layla, who was also making her way into the living room, in a short nicker and an underwear shirt, a telling look. Layla retreated from the living room not to be seen again throughout my stay that afternoon. Raliat in a black abayah sat on the same furniture as her mother and then the dreaded formalities began.

"Malik," Raliat's mother started, "since all these years, you didn't ask of me."

I tilted my head downwards, and mumbled, "It's not like that ma."

She laughed, and then asked, "how is it like then?"

Now I had no more answer in me so I kept quiet, trying to control the shaking of my legs. I began to feel cold from the inside.

"How are your parents?"

"They are fine, ma," I managed to reply. "Good," she commented.

The room became placid and then her voice rose again. "Raliat told me you both want to marry each other. Is that true?"

Marry each other! I raised my head to look at Raliat and I found her to be ducking her head as well.

"Yh…ye..yes, ma," I stuttered, finding my voice. She sighed, regarded Raliat and me, and said, "Marriage is not a joke. I hope you kids know what you're doing. God will make you each other's friend."

"Ameen," Raliat and I chorused.

"Malik, have you told your parents?"

"No, I haven't." Her eyes became wide. "You haven't?" Raliat's face also displayed surprise.

"I mean not entirely," I lied.

"Make sure you discuss it with them and get back to me, or better yet, tell your mom to call me."

"I will do that, ma."

She heaved from the couch and began to walk towards the kitchen. "What do you want to eat?" she asked, using her hand to pack her hair.

"Thank you, ma. I'm alright."

I went to Washington Square Park to clear my head that afternoon before returning home. I sat by the fountain and watched as the water gushed out incessantly. I looked at the birds roaming about the park, and how they flocked around a man with a grey beard in a brown blazer and worn out jeans, who dropped bread in pieces for them. I could not help but envy the freedom of some of the young couples, most of them around my age, showing affections toward each other. A girl with jet black long hair in an I LOVE NY shirt and a boy in a brown three quarter nicker and blue T-shirt put up their phone for a selfie as they joined their lips together. I suspected them to be tourists from Europe. I found myself thinking, will my parents be as reasonable as Raliat's mother?

I had somewhat tried to brush the issue with my mother even before visiting Raliat's mom— I didn't mention Raliat or anyone to her— I just asked her what she would do if I said I wanted to marry.

"Don't even say you want to get married now, let alone of what I would do. You will get married only after you have become a medical doctor."

That had been her terse answer so I knew another explosion was around the corner. I got home around seven thirty at night that Friday, went to mosque and prayed. Upon returning home I dealt my parents the blow.

I explained to them with the mellowest of voices why I needed and wanted to get married hoping that their hearts would be softened by oration. My father remained calm and collected, casting a strange but steady glance over me as I spoke. My mother had no surprises for me. She received it in the exact way I had thought. Hands flying in the air, Yoruba words I couldn't understand pouring from her mouth, and she lashed me with her eyes throughout, the way only Nigerian mothers could manage while yelling, *"mo de je'iiya lori omo yi o*—I suffered raising this child. *"*

I went to bed that night feeling a bit relaxed, relieved that I had told them.

My father did not go to work the next morning but my mother went to the hospital where she worked so we had the house to ourselves. I was in my room chatting with Raliat on WhatsApp, still in pajamas, when my father opened the door and walked in. I sat up on the bed and he gave me a weary smile.

"When was the last time you swept your room?" he sat at the foot of the bed.

"Hmm," I ran my hand over my hair, "I think three days ago."

"You think?" he chuckled. "If you will get married, then you need to man up, you know."

I changed the way I was sitting and sat well to evince my seriousness. "I know," I started, but he shut me up.

"No, you don't know yet. You think you know but you don't know. And I, as your father, will tell you the things you need to know." I sealed my lips and opened my ears.

"You see, son, marriage is one of the best things in life and I would hate to deny you of it even though you have come to us earlier than the time your mother and I anticipated but it is all good. I understand your hormones are probably making *takbir* every now and then so you feel the need for marriage. But you must know that marriage transcends the quenching of your sexual desires."

At that point I felt somehow embarrassed so I averted my gaze.

"Uh, see the groom feeling shy when he hears sex,'' he joked, pointing at me.

Of course I knew about sex, I was nineteen, but having my old man talk to me about it was different; and in an explicable way, nice.

"Once you get married," he resumed, "the word 'I' dies from your life and you start using 'we'. You must become selfless, always considering your wife before making any decision even if you feel the decision has nothing to do with her. Your financial, emotional, physical, and social burdens become interlocked with each other's. But with the right mindset and prayers to Allah, you should be fine."

We hugged after our talk and he patted me in the back. "Son, I'm proud of you. And we will support you and Raliat."

Later that day, in the afternoon, Raliat and I met at Washington Square Park. It was the first day we would sit and talk after our engagement. She preceded me to the park so she had to text me to know what part of the park she was at. I walked past the white arch to the right of the fountain and my gaze fell on her. She was attired in a black abayah, at the end of the sleeves ran gold color designs. A gold color hijab glittered on top.

I gasped. "Salaam alaykum,'' I greeted from the rear.

"Wa alaykum salaam," she turned her face.

I had to force myself not to stare at her during our talk; for she looked striking. I told her of my father's reaction, conveniently forgetting to mention that of my mother. We talked about a host of other things but something had changed about Raliat. The Raliat I knew since childhood had never been shy in front of me but on that day she couldn't even meet my gaze. And when she spoke, her voice was mellow. Something indelible happened before we left the park that afternoon. My mind had been on something else when I heard Raliat caught me off guard, "Malik, why did you propose to me?"

I rambled and rambled, and mumbled, but I couldn't get a coherent statement out. And if you still ask me now, I still can't. I don't know why I love Raliat.

That night I had a sudden craving for vanilla ice cream so I jumped out of bed and headed for the kitchen, but as I came down to the living room I saw my parents sitting by the freezer in apparently one of their *love in Tokyo* moods. This time they both sat on dining chairs but my mother's right foot was being massaged on my father's thighs. I found a place behind a wall to eavesdrop. The wall truly had ears that night.

"Jumoke, we have to support our son," my father said.

"I know, Sodiq, I know, but isn't he too young for marriage?"

My father exhaled and replied, "He is an intelligent boy. He is not too young. If he is not too young to have girlfriends, then he is certainly not too young to get married."

"But what about his school?" She asked.

"We've discussed about that this morning and it won't affect it."

"Okay o, Baba ati omo, you've discussed behind my back, *abi?*" she shot back.

"No, it's not like that. It's just that you know this is America, and we can't really stop him from doing anything, so I figured it is better we support him and Raliat and pray that Allah makes them each other's friend."

"I have heard," After a long silence, mother conceded.

"You have heard or you have agreed?"

"I have agreed and I am happy. At least one doesn't get angry at the increase of God's favor."

Her last statement was enough for me to sleep in peace.

Igbeyawo

The Carrying of a Bride

Our wedding ceremony was set for a month from that Saturday. If it was left to Raliat and me, we would have had the wedding that weekend, but it wasn't left to us; and so our parents took to task. At first, we objected to a fancy wedding but both my mother and Raliat's mother put axe on their heads—disagreed vehemently. Their arguments were essentially the same: they'd been helping others celebrate weddings, and now it was time for their friends to help them too. Raliat and I, after thinking it through, figured they were entitled to an exquisite wedding, so we happily granted them the pleasure to carry on. They'd been generous enough to allow us to marry at such a young age, so granting them an opportunity to throw an elaborate party seemed a pretty nice deal. Moreover, it was their money not ours. They would carry the stress, we would carry nothing. We were in fact stress free as the wedding day zoomed in except for one issue. Housing.

We couldn't afford to rent a studio in the free market unless we got a subsidized housing deal. We applied, but our application was thrown into a never ending waiting list. If we were to rent a studio on Raliat's salary, we would have very little money left for food and transportation. I hadn't gotten a job because I wanted to start school first so that I could have a stable schedule. And yes, for the first few months of our marriage, we depended solely on Raliat's income. To rent a room and share an apartment with a stranger was not an option; so for those three weeks, we brainstormed a lot. I was at Asalaatu a week before our wedding when Alhaji Fajengbesi asked me where Raliat and I would be living. I told him that we would live with my parents for the mean time before I secure a job. He must have heard the distress in my voice because he told me I didn't sound happy about that. I told him of our search for a studio and how the high prices had been chasing us away.

"Don't worry," he assured, patting my shoulder. "I have a basement studio vacant in my house. I will rent it to you. And as a gift for your wedding, the first three months, you don't need to pay rent." I didn't know what got into me but I hugged him tightly.

Our Nikkah took place inside the mosque of Al Irshad Muslim Society on a Thursday evening, a week before schools resumed for the fall semester. The mosque was full. I wore a white jallabiya and Raliat wore white abayah and a white hijab with black and brown design on it. Her tiny nose ring gleamed at me whenever I stared.

"Malik, have you given her *mahr*?" Imam Abdul Rahman asked.

I nodded that I had.

"Raliat, did you accept the *mahr*?"

"Yes, I did," Raliat answered in a low voice inaudible to the audience even with the aid of a microphone.

"Who is acting as the Wali overseeing this union?" he continued.

Raliat's maternal uncle who had come from Texas in his large white agbada and black gobi, a man of lanky stature and ebony look, stood and said he was the guardian.

"Malik, do you accept Raliat as your wife?"

I showed the whiteness of my teeth as a wide smile cleaved my lips. "Yes, I do."

"Takbeer!" a stout man encouraged, and the congregation chorused, "Allahu akbar—God is great!!"

When silence returned, Imam Abdul Rahman continued, "Raliat, do you take Malik as your husband?"

"Na'am," she replied in Arabic and the mosque roared 'Allahu akbar' again.

"O people in the mosque," Imam turned to the congregation, "bear witness that Raliat and Malik are now married under the eyes of Allah."

"Malik, hold your wife's hand," Imam Abdul Rahman commanded. And tears streamed down my face as I held Raliat's hand for the first time as her husband.

The wedding followed the next day. The venue was Concourse Village Hall at the intersection of 161st Street and Morris Avenue. The event commencement time on the invitation cards read four pm but the caterers and event designers didn't arrive until six pm. Even the bride made sure that six thirty clocked before arriving in a limousine. Eventually, the ceremony took off fifteen minutes short of seven o'clock. I really don't have the words to make the hall, atmosphere, taste, and smell of that evening vivid. The ceremony was just too colorful, beautiful and memorable for my words to do justice to. Our mothers tried! Nonetheless, I would dabble.

I wore white buba and sokoto lace and mantled upon them a big turquoise agbada made of *aso oke* fabric. My turquoise *gobi* cap pressed to the left side. Raliat had mild remonstrations with our mothers concerning her own outfit. They wanted her to dawn her face with make-ups and batter her hijab for *gele* made of *aso oke* which will be wrapped about her head but will lay bare her necklace and earrings. She dissented regarding both. After lengthy persuasion from both sides, a concession was made: she agreed to allow the makeup artist to work on her but she would use a turquoise scarf as her hijab and not gele. A long piece of the same turquoise *aso oke—ipele—* ran over her white iro and buba lace. We both sat on decorated chairs made of rich canes, over us were white and turquoise fabrics folded in decoration and balloons of the same colors.

Family and friends wore sky blue lace and on top of their heads were gele and caps of deep blue hue. Our parents wore grey lace and blue aso oke. My mother killed it by making her gele tower higher than others'; an action meant to evince her importance as the mother of the groom. The ceremony followed the Yoruba tradition of donating yams, *kolanuts*, palm-oil and other edible things as symbolic gifts to the bride's family. I was made to prostrate, lying down flat, chest touching the floor, a million times and Raliat knelt countless times, too. One time, I was called out, and was asked to tell the hall how we had met. I stuttered and the anchoress—*alaga'ijoko*, a light-skinned woman with a huge gele, akin to a ceiling fan on top her head, fined me forty dollars. I paid, family and friends also joined in paying. Another time, after we cut the cake, Raliat was told to feed me for the first time in front of attendees. She cut a morsel from the cake and fed me. She left the place thinking that was it, but the anchoress beckoned her back and said she had to complement it with a drink—ha! We did all sorts of funny things, and at the end I was told to carry my wife to show I was man enough to marry her. That was a bit hectic, but I managed to lift Raliat for a few seconds.

The day rained food in excess. White rice, fried rice, jollof rice, semolina, amala, pounded yam, chicken, beef, turkey were some of the items on the menu. Appetizers in form of salads, pepper soup, moin-moin, and deserts.

As an epilogue to anchoress' series of demands for embarrassing displays, she announced that it was time for the couple to dance. They couldn't find us. We had escaped while people were eating to pray

Maghrib in one of the empty spaces around the Concourse Village Hall.

At ten o'clock, while friends and families were still throwing it down on the dance floor, men waving their hands, stamping their feet, and women oscillating their hips, we were driven off to our studio apartment in a white limousine. We had initially resolved not to get all touchy-feely until we reach our apartment but in the duskiness of the limousine backseat, with no one watching, a light of different tint shinning over the roof, I gazed at the almond tone face of Raliat, and her thin soft lips incessantly appealed to me. I glued my lips on them, defying our resolution, and I found Raliat a willing accomplice.

We stood for some minutes under the moonlight, waving at Layla and a cousin of Raliat as they hopped back into the long stretched car. Raliat and I, hands intertwined, stood on the lawn, and watched as the limousine melted into the darkness of the night. We looked at each other and we both smiled. "Bismillah, let's go inside," I prompted.

We had already set up our apartment a week before. But prior to the wedding, our insisting mothers hired help to make sure it was befitting enough for their stature. Their efforts paid off though; the studio looked nice, neat and smelt great, like rose cologne. I was not tired but I needed a warm bath. We took turns: after my bath, Raliat also went to the bathroom. I had just finished praying when she came out, walking slowly, her crimson towel laying bare her glowing chocolate body and silhouetting her hips and succulent bosom. My head flew.

I stood for Isha' prayer and Raliat prayed behind me. After the prayer, I sat on the bed and engaged myself in dhikr. Raliat now in a transparent night gown came to sit beside me and untied her hijab, revealing the red beads on her braids. She dropped the hijab on my thighs. I took that at face value (In Yoruba culture that's usually an appeal) so I rounded my hands about her waist. I tilted my head towards her and she pushed me back gently. "No, the two rakah first," she winked. I jumped up, and we quickly got the two rakah over with. I stood over her as she was on the praying mat and put my hand on her head, and then read the supplication of the newlyweds.

We were facing each other, standing, my jallabiya brushing her abayah, when I saw concern in her eyes. Her lips began to move and I pressed my index finger on them, discontinuing her from speaking. When love descends, words are, sometimes, needless. I held on to her arms and felt her hand around my waist. My eyes closed and our lips embraced, heralding the best night of my life.

Iyanu l'aiye

A Wonderful World

I see trees of green, red roses too
I see them bloom for me and you
And I think to myself what a wonderful world.

It was at dawn on Monday. I had just returned from a small mosque close to our apartment. I sat on the bed, scrolling through my Facebook newsfeed. The shower noise stopped, bathroom door accentuated sounds suggesting unlocking, and after a few seconds, Raliat emerged draped in a short towel. She walked towards the dressing mirror, water dripping from her hair and her feet leaving wet spots on the rug. She sat on a stool and began to cream her arms. I walked over and stood behind her. We looked at our reflections in the mirror and a wide grin creased Raliat's lips. I ran my hands over her arms and gently pulled her up. Her braids touched my cheek as my hands wrapped her in a tight embrace.

Still looking at each other's reflections in the mirror, I put my hand on her bosom, caressing, and she smiled after a soft gasp. "Raliat, you're so beautiful," I whispered, my mouth touching her earlobe.

"Don't flatter yourself," she said, and then turned to face me. Before I could say anything else, she grabbed my head, her grip somewhat stern, and began to kiss me.

Later that day, around noon, we went to the Presbyterian Church on West 56th Street, between 5th Avenue and Broadway. Raliat had registered for volunteering before our wedding; so after showering together at eleven thirty, she started dressing up. I realized I couldn't bear the thought of not seeing her for a few hours so I decided to go with her. As we reached the side of the church, Raliat asked two men who looked like contractors in their dirty jeans and yellow helmets if they knew where the entrance to the Food on Wheels program kitchen was.

"Right here." One of the men pointed to a red side door which looked rusty. It was rugged and looked as though no one had used it in a decade. "When you get in, turn to your left and take the staircase to the basement," he concluded at the same time his cigarette pack coming out of his pocket.

"Thank you," Raliat and I chorused, then we used the side door as advised.

The basement was large. It was not just a kitchen; there was a spacious cafeteria in it where people of advanced age sat, ate, and socialized. The place smelt of lettuce and wheat. I followed Raliat's lead through the condensed tables; being mindful of the people whose body couldn't handle a trip or fall. As I walked behind her, I noticed her black long skirt hugged her mildly; and the frame of her jutting hips magnified in my eyes. I took a mental note of mentioning the tightness of the skirt to her sometime later. Nonetheless, I loved that she had chosen to wear it under her yellow silk blouse. Raliat opened her arms and a white lady, who seemed to be in her early twenties, filled the space.

"You made it, Raliat," she said in a southern accent.

"I did, right?" Raliat exclaimed, faking a surprise face. They released each other and then turned to me. "This is Malik, my husband," she pointed, almost laughing. "And this is Rebecca," she touched the lady's shoulder.

Rebecca stretched her hand, but my hands remained buried in my pockets, I smiled and dropped my head. Raliat quickly held her hand and wangled it in a playful manner. "We don't shake hands with the opposite sex," Raliat explained.

We were assigned to deliver foods to elders who, for one reason or the other, couldn't make it to the cafeteria. The sheet on the clipboard read seven names, each with its address and telephone number. The first delivery was for an old woman whom it was written beside her name on the clipboard 'Limited Hearing.' Yet she was supposed to buzz us in. When we reached the door to her apartment building, we called her four times before she picked up. And we had to explain to her seven times before the buzzing sounded. We knocked at her door countless times before she opened. She was not old, no. She was old age itself. Her yellow hair was frail, her white gown was frail, and wrinkles covered her face. I was overcome with emotions. I stared at her face, looking to see remnants of her youthful days; I wanted to see if those days of red lipstick, of firm lips, of pointed nose, of blond hair still remained behind the surface. I put the green bag down and took out a vegetarian sandwich and banana. Raliat took them from me and gave it to the woman who gave a silent nod.

"Is everything alright, Mrs. Maynard? Or do you need anything else?" Raliat asked, as I closed the green bag and stood up.

"What?" Mrs. Maynard asked.

"I asked is everything fine?"

Mrs. Maynard eyes widened in enthusiasm but she still couldn't hear Raliat.

"You have to talk louder," she said gently, at the same time tilting her head towards Raliat.

Raliat moved her mouth closer to her left ear, "Are you fine, Mrs. Maynard? That's what I am asking, how are you feeling?" A wide smile of joy and melancholy overtook her mouth and she blushed, or so it seemed.

"At ninety-eight, what do you think?" she asked, and silence filled the air. "Thank you a lot for bringing my food. God bless you."

We delivered the rest of the foods to the others except two who neither answered their phones nor opened their doors. They were all old, and extremely so. I had thought prior getting there that we were going to be giving food to some poor old people but I had been wrong. The people we gave food to all lived in luxurious apartment buildings in the heart of Manhattan, one of the costliest places to live on the planet, and yet they would starve if such a humanitarian service was not available. Amidst the hectic and fast lives of New Yorkers, how many would think of a woman of ninety eight, inside an exquisite building in Manhattan, nursing hunger of food and companionship.

We returned to the church and told Rebecca that we couldn't deliver food to two of the seven people. She said it was fine and that it happened many times. They would send people to check on them again later. We took a selfie together, and Raliat told Rebecca to send it to her phone. We walked to the train station and took the 2 train then later on transferred to the Harlem bound 3 train as we decided to pay Raliat's mother a visit in her hair braiding salon.

From the outside, I already saw through the glass door that there were no clients inside. It was only Raliat's mother and her coworker who were in the salon watching TV. I opened the door, held it steadily, and Raliat took a step into the salon. I followed. And both Raliat's mother and the coworker, a middle aged lady of vigorous frame and shinning dark complexion, rushed towards us and pressed us with embraces.

"Husband and wife!" They shouted, and burst into laughter.

Then I became extremely shy. I wanted to run out of the store right then.

"Malik, how are you guys?" Auntie Abeni, the coworker, asked placing an emphatic tone on the 'how' and then winked. I knew what she was getting at, so I responded only by smiling.

We were entertained with juice and fried plantains. Raliat and Auntie Abeni did the talking, I just kept my head bowed the entire time. We spent thirty minutes at the salon and then set out, but not before Auntie Abeni told us to be on our kneels as she prayed for us.

We propelled toward downtown on the 3 train because Raliat had some issues to sort out at the financial aid office of the Borough of Manhattan Community College. We got off at the Park Place Station and walked toward Greenwich Street where the sight of the freedom tower was clear to view. Right close to it stood the Fiterman Hall, a building endowed to BMCC by Shirley Fiterman. Raliat had once told me the building suffered heavily alongside the twin towers during the horrific attacks of September 11 and that it had recently opened after years of construction. I gazed at the tallest building in the western hemisphere and I thought of the people who lost their lives that grim morning and those who have continued to lose their lives, properties and families as a result of the decisions made at the wake of the attacks.

A group of tourists walked up to us and asked if we knew where the 9/11 Memorial Museum was. Raliat pointed the direction to them, and they hurried towards a pleasure birthed from intense pain; and more so, they were willing to pay for the spectacle.

We climbed up the sloped spacious entrance of the 199 Chamber Street campus, the sun leaving shadows behind us. I held one of the entrance door opened for Raliat and another lady whose hands held folders tightly to the chest. By the right of the door, on the wall, the names of eight faculty members of BMCC who lost their lives during that morning of terror.

Raliat swiped her ID at the turnstile while I showed my ID and pressed the last four digit on my social security card number at the security counter. We took the escalator to the third floor and walked across an internal bridge to the northern side of the building. The view of the Hudson River, provided by the internal bridge, was marvelous. A student sat near the transparent glass, his head fixed on the textbook in his hand. Two men and three ladies, in weird clothes and funky hairstyles, clamped at a corner, arguing about Meek Mill and Drake. Just over their heads, on the wall, on a blue poster was written: *Sshhhh! This is a quiet lounge. Enjoy the view....*

I hurried behind Raliat down the staircase of Chambers Street subway station; and just before the 2 train's doors closed, we jumped in and sat beside each other as we headed uptown towards our home. Raliat sat close to the end of the seat so that her arms touched the handrails, and a white man with heavy, long white beard sat beside me.

"Sa—la—mu— alaiku," he greeted in a strange accent.

I responded.

"Are you shocked that I greeted you like that?" he asked, his eyes twinkling behind his round glasses. "Oh no," I lied.

We both kept quiet for a few seconds, then I asked if he was a Muslim.

"No, I am not a Muslim, but I saw that you're a Muslim and I wanted to ask you something."

I looked at him in confusion, and asked, "How do you know I'm a Muslim?"

He smiled. "When you're old as I am, you will be able to spot new husbands and wives. Isn't she your wife?" I smiled and nodded. "So what's your question?"

"What's the real position of Mohammed in Islam? Is he like God's partner or something?" he asked.

"Well, Muhammad, according to us," I started, "is the last prophet and messenger of God. He is not a partner of God. He was just a man like us. He ate, drank, and lived like other human beings, but the difference is that he was chosen by God to be the last among the series of…. You know, Abraham, Moses, Noah and Jesus, according to Islam, were all prophets and messengers of Islam, Muhammad just happened to be the final one. He is a servant of God. It is just the he was chosen to deliver the message of salvation to humanity."

"I see," he nodded.

In the hope that he wouldn't ask more questions, as my knowledge of interreligious discourse wasn't that great, I asked if he was a Christian.

"Oh no," he shook his head, "I am not religious. I am spiritual. I believe in humanity, you could say I am a humanist."

I smiled and said, "Well, I'm religious and I am also spiritual. And I am a Muslim and I feel empathy, and I'd like to see a more peaceful and just world. Aren't I by that a humanist too?"

He smiled and I saw his canine teeth. It was his stop. We shook hands and he got out of the car.

I surveyed the faces and body expressions of fellow New Yorkers inside the train car. Two black women sat opposite each other and talked about a third friend who would not leave her abusive boyfriend. A young Latino and Latina held hands and continued to stare at each other with love. A sitting elderly white lady rested her hands on her walker. Two white men in corporate suits cross checked things on a paper. A Chinese lady held two grocery bags and leaned on the door.

Louis Armstrong's beautiful voice rose in my mind and I thought what possibly could have led him to write down such a brilliant poetry and turned it into a touching song. Was he in the woods? Was he driving? Was he out on a farm? Was he looking down the earth from a mountain top? Or was he at some place in North Africa in the deserts? I wanted to know what force or forces drove him to a deep contemplation of this world. He must have been inspired by the natural, not artificial. And this is evinced in the lyrics itself. He wasn't talking about cars, he wasn't amazed at the tallness of the empire state building, and he was not astounded by the engineering genialness which brought about subways. Rather, he looked at the horizon and saw the skies of blue and clouds of white; the bright blessed day, the dark sacred night; the colors of the rainbow so pretty in the sky; but he also saw people going by, as we were among these beautiful creations of God he thought of. He saw friends shaking hands saying how do you do, but they were really saying I love you. Then he heard babies cry, and he watched them grow. And the verses came to him.

I looked at my Raliat,
and she was already asleep
Her head on my shoulder,
and her hands on my thighs.

Then I thought to myself
What a wonderful world
What a wonderful world.

Odun Meta to koja

The Last Three Years

The last three years have been the best years of my life in every way. Many times when I sit and reflect about the favors and blessings I have received during these past years, I couldn't shake the feeling that marrying Raliat had simply been an opening to great things. The Qur'an says: *...Live with women kindly, for if you dislike them, you're disliking people through which God brings lots and lots of good things.* Raliat and I lived with love and understanding and we reaped its ample benefits. Our marriage seemed like an impetus to the waves of achievements encircling us from all sides.

First, shortly after our wedding, Raliat was granted the Out in Two scholarship at Borough of Manhattan Community College. Thus she received grants for each of her last three semesters. Also during the same semester, her job union started paying for three of her courses, so the school refunded to her one thousand and five hundred dollars every semester. That wasn't all. I started tutoring at Hunter College and also worked a part time job. By the time the spring semester came, I got accepted for a full scholarship at Hunter College, and also received grants from a number of other scholarships. We now had more than enough. We were showered grants from all ends: Pell, TAP, Out In Two, CSEA, Hunter Foundation and several other grants. I stopped working part time and focused more on school. I also began an internship at NYU Lutheran Medical Center in Brooklyn. On a financial level, we were blessed. It was as though we were being paid for going to school. However, we had to play our part—the grades we made sure stayed up.

Many a day on train rides, I would fall asleep out of fatigue, dropping my head in whatever book I might be reading. There was this train ride I can't forget: I had had three exams that day and typed lots of emails in response to hospital clients, so by the time I hobbled down the dark chamber of Chambers Streets train station, I had been profoundly exhausted. As I entered into the brightly lit 2 express train, I found a seat by a lady who looked like she was from the Caribbean; lips painted in red, and a heap of artistically woven dreadlocks sat on her head. The next thing, I woke up to find my head on her shoulder.

"I'm sorry." I apologized.

"It's okay. Long day?" She grinned.

Often times at school I would get eyebrows raised at me and the dropping of jaws thanks to the ring on my finger.

"You're married?" I would grin in response.

"How old are you?" That question I came to decipher as mere rhetoric.

"Gosh! You're so young. You should be enjoying life now!"

And this I couldn't help but ponder on what exactly they meant. Enjoying life? Did I tell them I was suffering? Or who petitioned their unsolicited pity in the first place? To me, there is no enjoyment purer, lasting, and more organic and of spiritual benefit than to return home after a stressful day at school or work to the caressing arms of one's spouse. Raliat's welcome kiss at night—regardless of who gets home first— was an antidote to the strains of the outside world.

Two months to the spring semester, without eating too much, Raliat's stomach began to protrude and we waited anxiously for it to shrink. During the cold early days of fall, when green leaves turned yellow, and moist covered the atmosphere, her jut stomach returned to being flat and we welcomed two precious gifts—Azeez and Azeezat—from God. I had just finished a test when my phone rang and my mom told me to come down to the hospital as Raliat was in labor. I rushed to the hospital and when I got there, I was given a scrub to wear as though I had already become a doctor. I was thrust into the labor room to witness the result of my well-intended gestures of affection on one of the January nights when the sky was umber, and the roads were covered in bleached heaps of frozen moisture which had whipped the earth during the afternoon blizzard. I was cold and she was shivering so we thought it prudent to help each other out.

We were in the labor room for about six hours. It was a bit hard. Raliat had decided to go natural. But finally around seven o'clock at night the contractions became frequent and the 'pushing' started. I couldn't bear to watch helplessly as my wife groaned and moaned in pain, so I helped her out by crying. O' yes, I cried. I wept. In fact, I cried more than the twins did. My respect for women had always been huge, but after that day, my respect for women increased exponentially, transcending any possible imagination.

Our babies brought more light and happiness into our home. Numerous times after dealing with the tumult of the outside world, I would return home feeling down but as soon as I gazed at Azeez and Azeezat, a feeling of ease and joy would sweep over me. That feeling when I carry my babies and look into their eyes, and in their eyes is something that tells me everything is going to be fine. People say marriage is not a bed of roses. This might be true as the rule, but to every rule is an exception; Raliat and I were exceptions. We showed nothing to each other but love. Of course we seldom had moments of disagreement, but those moments were always in turn channeled into boosting our love. If we disagreed, and I knew I was wrong, I knew how to apologize whilst still keeping that stupid thing called male pride. A hug from the rear coupled with a kiss on the neck and followed with whispering 'I love you and I'm sorry' into her ear. And we were back in each other's arms. The next night, I would make sure to take the garbage out before she mentioned it. If she was the one who was wrong, well, I like her penance better. My favorite meal and a *sleep-less* night.

Raliat transferred to City College after graduating from Borough of Manhattan Community College. Because of her interest in psychology and sociology, she yielded to the advice of one of her professors at BMCC and applied for CUNY Baccalaureate Unique and Interdisciplinary Studies. She was accepted and thus had access to classes all over the City University of New York's colleges. She now had one semester left to obtain her baccalaureate degree in Social Psychology and Religious Ethics. As for me, four weeks ago, I received a letter of acceptance from Columbia University College of Physicians and Surgeons.

By this time the day before yesterday, I was in gaiety as we graduates walked down the stage in our graduation gowns and hats. We threw our hats up and posed in elation for several selfies with families and friends. I was outside the graduation hall with my parents, Raliat and Layla when my vision became blurred and my head increased in throbbing. I saw a reddish thick liquid pelt my black shoe and when I rubbed the back of my hand on my nose, my hand became stained with blood. My knees grew weak, and when it couldn't support me anymore, I heard my body thud on the pavement. *...call nine one-one...* a voice screamed distantly.

I woke up and found myself dressed in a patient gown inside what obviously was a hospital room.

"He is awake." I heard an African American lady in a white scrub announce to two doctors walking down the hallway.

They headed back and began to explain things to me but I told them I wanted to see my family first. In a little time, Raliat, my father and mother walked in. Raliat must have been crying a lot as her eyes were red. I told them I was fine and they need not worry.

This afternoon, Raliat came to the hospital and brought me fresh clothes to wear on the day I would be discharged. She also brought my favorite meal:

semolina and ewedu. She wore the white abayah I bought her as *mahr* and she looked more relaxed and beautiful than yesterday. It was apparent that she had lined her eyelashes with kohl (antimony) and glossed her lips with lipstick.

"My doctors said I am allergic to beauty, do you want to kill me?" I joked. She gave out a faint smile. "Raliat, I'm fine," I assured her.

I asked about Azeez and Azeezat and she said they were with my mother. We were saying something about clothes when the playlist on my laptop jumped to her favorite nasheed: ...*In shaa Alaah, In shaa Allah*... the lyrics permeated the room and she began to dance with her head. "You wanna dance, sister?" I asked, standing up from the bed and leading her to the floor. Her hands wrapped around my shoulder, and my hands on her hips, we enjoyed the moment, moving gently to the tune.

After the dance, we ate together and talked more. Then I led her in Asr prayer. After the prayer, I felt like sleeping, and she said she had to go and be with the twins as my mom would go to work. I was lying in the bed when she got ready to leave so she came near to the bed and tilted her head and kissed me.

"I love you," she declared.

I waited for her to stand straight and then replied, "I love you more."

Atipo la'je l'aiye
We're refugees in this world

It was on a Wednesday night. After dropping off Azeez and Azeezat at my mother's shop, Malik and I went on a romantic dinner to celebrate our wedding anniversary. The restaurant was on the corner of Madison and East Forty-Third Street; it was exquisite, well lit, and had delicious foods, too. I wore a black and yellow Ankara dress, and I wrapped the ankara fabric scarf about my head, then covered the scarf with a dainty black hijab, and clipped it firmly with a fancy hijab brooch. Malik wore a tuxedo suit but without the bow tie. He left the uppermost buttons unbuttoned. Beside our table was a large aquarium which gave us the pleasure of watching the fishes inside play.

"Raliat, thank you."

I furrowed my brows, suspended the fork on the lobster in my plate and asked what the thanks was for.

"For believing in me, for marrying me."

My face grew warm and butterflies flew in different directions inside me. That guy sure knew how to get to me. I fixed my gaze on the glass cup housing a few ounces of cider.

"I love you Malik," I said between giggles. He then leaned forward, still sitting, and I tilted my head, and our lips touched.

"I can't get that project off my mind," Malik said as he continued to pat my hair later that night, both of us lying on our backs on the bed.

He had been trying to raise funds for the internally displaced people who had lost their homes and livelihoods as a result of the monstrosities of Boko Haram in Nigeria but he hadn't been successful. Malik had lots of humanitarian projects in his head which often made him restless, so I wanted to let him know that he need not be overwhelmed and that he still had lots of years to do that.

"Sweetie pie," I started, wrapping my arm around his stomach which made his body tremble lightly.

"Calm down. You still have a whole life ahead of you."

He placed his hand on my arm, rubbed it gently, and asked, "Who told you that I have a whole life ahead of me?"

I remained quiet, contemplating on his rhetorical question.

"Raliat, our lives are in the hands of God, we're nothing but a bunch of refugees in this world."

I slept that night with a tinge of sadness in my mind, pondering on how ephemeral this worldly life is.

I had just tucked the twins to bed and made wudu' for the Witr prayer when the hospital's caller ID showed on my phone. When I picked the phone, it was the voice of Malik's doctor. I should come as soon as possible. I tied my brown scarf, got ready, and dialed Layla's phone. She should come and watch over the twins. I called Malik's father and then took a cab to the hospital. The doctor led us to a different room, where I saw Malik lay on the bed in what seemed a deep sleep. The silence in the room was deafening and intuitively I knew something was wrong. The lights were on but dimmed. The white cloth covered his body save the head. I walked to the bed and leaned towards my love and the reality fell upon me. I was staring at the lifeless body of my soul mate. Tears streamed down my face, dropping on the white cloth covering Malik's body. Just like that. My Malik was dead. It felt surreal; like a dream. No, no! It couldn't be. But it was real. I looked at him on the bed and he didn't look dead. He looked like he was sleeping. He looked really relaxed. I bent and kissed his cheek and I found it cold. I rose, sniffled and then the tears let loose. I wanted him to stand up and tell me everything was fine, but he wouldn't, he couldn't.

I sat outside the room on the floor, my back reclining against the wall, eyes closed, and Malik's smiles, dimples, jokes, hugs, kisses all paid me visits. We had just eaten together and danced that afternoon, not knowing it was all a farewell. My mother came later that night, and when she embraced me, my head swelled even more, and I wet her dress with tears.

The next morning as we got the necessary paperwork done, one of Malik's doctors, a white man with a bald head and countenance reeking of pores and wrinkles, took out a white note and handed it to me with an apologetic expression. "I'm sorry for your loss," he murmured as he walked away. I opened it and tears immediately blurred my vision as I read the fine handwritings of my love.

Sweetheart,

I had a dream where I saw a man whose face was bright as the sun. The man was standing by a river and he told me to drink from it. When I drank from the river, I felt good. I don't think I'm coming back home, so please do these things for me:

Keep my privacy, and be the one to bathe me.

I have written an account of the summer we married on my laptop, please publish it.

And most importantly, please raise our children with Islam. Raliat, I love you, and marrying you has been the most precious and wisest decision I have ever made. May we meet again in Jannah

With love,

Malik.

I kept my husband's privacy and made the ritual cleansing of him in the funeral home. It was difficult, but I knew I had to fulfill his will. I wasn't afraid of bathing him, it was the emotions which made it difficult. I fought back tears as I passed water over him on the white broad funeral table the following morning. Later in the afternoon, he was driven to the Muslim cemetery in New Jersey, and thus my *Iddah* began.

Two days later, a prayer session was held for him in his parents' house where I passed my *Iddah*. People from Asalaatu poured into the house, some standing when all the seats had been occupied. Imam Abdul Rahman gave a sermon where he praised Malik for leading a good life and doing the right thing even when the society said otherwise. He urged me and Malik's parents to bear the pains with patience in the hope that God would reward us for our loss.

During the prayer session, I sat with my mother on whose lap Azeez sat, playing. Azeezat sat on Malik's mother's thighs, her arms wrapped over Azeezat. As I gazed at Malik's parents, I wondered how bitter it would have been for them had they forbidden us from marrying—they would have been left stripped off of any comfort by the death of their only child. Medical school wouldn't have mattered anymore. And a Cornell degree would have been rendered useless. The Imams pointed to my children as gifts from God to console all of us whom Malik had left behind in this world. But for me, Malik's life and the times we spent together, were already enough of a consolation.

...and then We bring you forth as infants; then We nourish you so that you may reach the age of full strength. There are some of you who die young......then most surely, you shall be raised back to life again on the Day of Resurrection.

— Qur'an, Surah Al Hajj: 5; Surah Al Mu'minun: 12

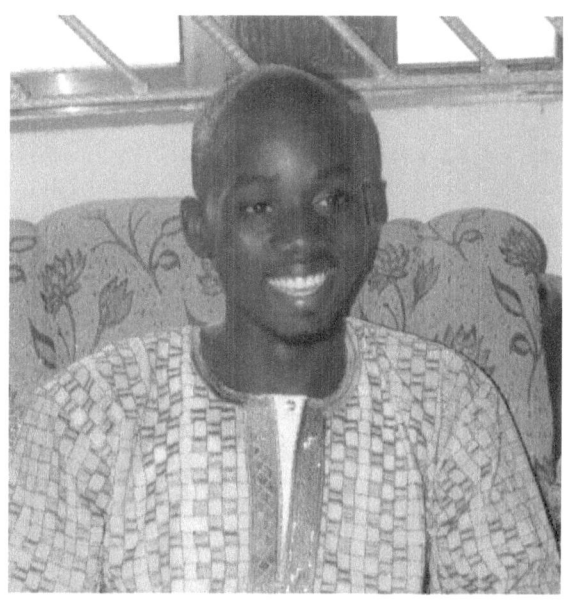

Find Adejumo's short stories:
www.tohibadejumo.com
Find Tohib Adejumo on Facebook:
https://www.facebook.com/toyeeb.aladejumo
Contact: tohibadejumo@gmail.com